T0132163

Debra Jones

The pain of love

POOKIE BLUFFINI

iUniverse, Inc.
Bloomington

Debra Jones
The Pain of Love

iUniverse books may be ordered through booksellers or by contacting:

iUniverse
1663 Liberty Drive
Bloomington, IN 47403
www.iuniverse.com
1-800-Authors (1-800-288-4677)

*Because of the dynamic nature of the Internet, any web addresses or links
contained in this book may have changed since publication and may no longer be
valid. The views expressed in this work are solely those of the author and do not
necessarily reflect the views of the publisher, and the publisher hereby disclaims
any responsibility for them.*

*Any people depicted in stock imagery provided by Thinkstock are models,
and such images are being used for illustrative purposes only.*

Certain stock imagery © Thinkstock.

ISBN: 978-1-4620-0181-1 (sc)
ISBN: 978-1-4620-0182-8 (ebook)

Printed in the United States of America

iUniverse rev. date: 3/7/2011

THE INTRODUCTION

―――――――――

This a story about a lady who lost her husband in Iraq. She has a tough time moving on but tries when she finds a clean cut man from up north that she really thinks she know until its almost too late. Her name is Debra Jones and she grew up around a loving family that loves her so much that they get involve and learns a that her new man has a past that he tries to cover up. She's also a devoted mother of a precious daughter name Morgan who looks up to her and a brother name Robert that Debra adores. Debra was older than Robert but he was very protective over her. And Debra always looks to her crazy cousin Sherry for advice on life. Sherry was a mother also but enjoyed the party life.

The man Debra falls in love with is a small business man that is very successful. His name is Allen. A very clean cut man with charm that could persuade a preacher's wife to commit adultery. But there is something fishy about this gentleman that even the most anointed priest couldn't figure out.

This story was inspired by a woman I seen on a talk show who couldn't escape an abusive husband. It touched me in a way that I can't explain in words. So I hope you enjoy this story as much as I did writing it. I also wrote this story because it is the total opposite of the lyrics I write for my albums. I really hope you enjoy the story and if so look for my other stories that will be out soon.

THANK YOUS

First off I have to thank God. My crazy mother Miss Sherry Hill, my uncle Joe Loc, my brother Popeye, my sisters Punkin, Leslie, and Erica hope you find this girl. My aunts, Maple, and Tutu. The Boyd's, Ricardo, Rikisha, Orlando, Ricky, and Nick thanks for rolling with a crazy dude like me. Kristen what you cooking tonight girl. Waldo thanks for those long nights working on album covers and now books. Willy Mullins let's put out that Ms P'ches album. Black Male we going to blow up even if it takes a few more years. To Big Phil also known as Kujo Spacino you truly are family. To my kids you brats are my inspiration. Anisha thank you for the covers baby. Tabatha Bramlett thank you for staying cool with me. To my nieces and nephews your uncle Pookie is here and got your back. To my cousins y'all can always hit me up. To all of my friends I did time with in prison because you fools kept me laughing in those dark times in the bricks. Shay Montgomery was the finest girl in the Bluff and gave me an idea of true beauty. To Bobby Buck keep working hard. Hey Fat Allen Fair stay out the pen bro. To the ones I forgot get the next one.

CHAPTER ONE

After the funeral at Debra's house everyone brought food. A kid was running around playing and the adults were reminiscing on the good times. Debra looked at her mom with a face full of tears. I miss him so much" said Debra". I know baby, I know "her mother cried". Why he had to go so soon momma" Debra replied". God ways are mysterious Debby "her mom replied". How did you make it when daddy died momma "Asked Debra"? Child it wasn't easy but God pulled me through "her mother replied". I know momma I just wish my faith was as strong as yours "Debra replied". It will baby because I raised you on the word of God, that's why I know you will be fine "her mother added".

Pastor Mike walks in the den where Debra and her mother were. Hello ladies "he greeted". Hey Pastor "they replied". I know its tuff Debby but God has his reasons "said Pastor Mike". I know Pastor I just wish I knew his reasons "said Debra". Are you going to be ok Debby "Asked Pastor Mike"? I'll make it pastor; I'll make it "she replied". Well I think we should pray that God give us peace and walk us through these dark times Debbie "said Pastor Mike". Do you think prayer would help and would you pray with me

Debbie "asked Pastor Mike"? Well pastor I think we all need prayer "she replied". Amen to that "he added". He called more people in the room to join his prayer circle including her mother. Let's bow our heads and close our eyes "said the pastor as he began the prayer.

Father God gives us the understanding and strength through these hard times with wisdom and knowledge as we continue to study your word. Father you told us you would never leave or forsake us. And you are a just God. Lord, though we are not worthy of your blessings you love us so much that you sent your only begotten Son to die for our sins. So I'm coming to you to ask please look over Debby as she walk this dark journey that the evil one is lurking to catch your followers when they are weak. But Lord I know you we will see that she prevail and leave old slew foot defeated in Jesus name we pray Amen.

Thanks pastor I really needed that and it did make me feel a lot better "said Debra". Oh no Debby not me, the glory is all God "Pastor Mike replied". You better fix you some of that good food in there Debby "said Pastor Mike". I will pastor "she replied". The pastor leaves the room and heads for the kitchen. Debra walked toward the window and just stared outside and began to pray to herself. Her mom walks in the room and gently grabs her right hand. Baby I know it hurt and I wish I could take the pain away but you must give it to God Debby "her mother cried". I know momma I just wish I could have at least told him goodbye and tell him how much I love him "said Debby". Debra's daughter Morgan walks in the room.

Mommy is daddy coming back "asked Morgan"? No sweetie he's not "Debra replied". Why did God take my daddy momma "asked Morgan"? Baby God have to take people so he'll have people to talk to up there honey "answered Debra". But I need daddy with us momma "said

Morgan". I know sweetie he's watching over us now baby "said Debra". He sure is, now let's go eat "her mother added". Ok grandma "said Morgan". Thanks mom I'll be there in a minute "said Debra". Ok Debby, I'll feed Morgan. Thanks mother. Debra went in her room and set on her bed staring at a picture of her ex husband.

Debra went to a local jazz bar with her little brother name Robert that she called RJ. Thanks for coming RJ "said Debra". Anything for my big sis "Robert replied". I can't believe we buried James today "said Debra". I know sis it totally caught me off guard too "said Robert". Morgan is taking it a lot harder than I thought she would "Debra added".

James was one of the best person I've ever met "said Robert". He was a sweetheart wasn't he "laugh Debra". Debra face lit up with a big smile as she remembers the good times with her beloved James. You only drinking "asked Robert"? You better put some food in you sis "he added. I really don't have an appetite right now "she replied". You got to eat something Debby "said Robert". I know RJ but I'm just not hungry right now "said Debra". I know sis I'm just worried about you "said Robert". I know RJ but I'm a big girl now "she replied". Do you need me to keep Morgan this week end "asked Robert"? Nah I'm cool RJ "she answered". I'm sorry sis but I'm not taking no for an answer "Robert laugh". Alright RJ you win "Debra replied". That'll give you a little time to yourself to relax and think "said Robert". Yeah I guess RJ "she whispered". Plus Morgan will love to play with her cousins and it'll help her to deal with the matter too "Robert added". Yeah she would love that RJ "said Debra". Plus momma will get her Sunday for church "Robert added". I know how momma is about her church "laughs Debra".

Moments later their cousin sherry joins them at the table. Hi y'all "yelled Sherry". Hey what's up CiCi "shouted Robert"? Sherry what are you doing here girl, you are supposed to be at work "shouted Debra". Girl I called in from work and I'm sorry about James "said Sherry". I'm ok girl but you are going to lose your job "Debra replied". Well I had to see y'all in these tuff times. Girl where are your kids "asked Robert"? With their daddy, now Debby we are going clubbing once you get yourself together "said sherry". I don't do clubs CiCi and don't you have a man "asked Debra". So what he don't know won't hurt him "said Sherry". You are so silly "laughs Debra". Silly is not the word for her 'added Robert". The three enjoyed the night by talking and laughing about the good old days. And Debra felt very

Confident around her close family members like nothing could harm her as long as she had them on her side. And she knew the next chapter in her life would heavily involve them. Now she just prays that this part of her life will pass and the good times will be knocking at her door.

CHAPTER TWO

A week later on a warm Friday morning at Debra's house the alarm clock is beeping. Morgan get up you have school and we are running late "yelled Debra". Let that child alone I'll take her to school her "mother replied". Are you sure mother "asked Debra"? Yeah child I already have her dressed "her mother answered". Ok she have to brush her teeth, wash her face "said Debra". Oh sugar it's not my first rodeo "her mom laughs". I know mother, I'm sorry "said Debra". That's ok just get ready for work Debby before you are late "her mother replied". Oh I saw Sherry last night mother "said Debra". That crazy niece of mine was suppose to been working last night "her mother replied". Yeah momma you know how she is "laughs Debra". That girl goes through men like water "her mother added". Debra laughs like she just heard the funniest joke ever. I'm serious Debby "her mom says with a serious look on her face". You're so silly mother "said Debra". So is RJ keeping Morgan next week "her mother asked". Yes he thinks it will be good for her so I'm ok with whatever helps her. That boy can put up a fight just like his dad "mother added". Yeah dad was a true fighter "replied Debra". Ain't that the truth "said mother". I can use the time to either read or go watch a movie. Don't worry about Morgan because she will be fine with her cousins "mothered added". The phone rings. Debra picks up and answers "hello". What's up girl "shouted Sherry"! CiCi it's 7:30 in the morning "answerer Debra". I want you to go to the club with me tonight "yelled Sherry". I told you how I feel about the club scene girl "said Debra". Well I'll be there at 8:30 tonight girl, later "said Sherry" then she hung up. Momma this girl just calls to torment me "laughs Debra". Yeah she doesn't have a lick of sense "said mother". Well I'm gone momma, you take care and I love you "said Debra". I love you too Debby her "mother replied".

Later after Debra gets off work she learns RJ is in her home. RJ what are you doing here "asked Debra"? Nothing trying to find some CD's "he answered" . Anyways how is Morgan doing "she asked"? She's good just playing with her cousins, now just enjoy the alone time "Robert replied". I know she's ok I'm just worried about her "said Debra". She's ok Debby; she's with family now helping me find some R&B "Robert replied". Anyways that crazy cousin of tours is stopping by "said Debra". I hope I'm gone when she get here "replied Robert". She's not that bad RJ "Debra laughs". Ok she's loud, rude, and obnoxious, should I say more "he added". Ok maybe she is that bad but she is still family "said Debra". Only by blood "said Robert". Well CiCi is CiCi "she laughs". So what are y'all doing tonight "asked Robert"? She says we're going clubbing but I don't know "she replied". Definitely not a good idea with that crazy girl "Robert added". That crazy girl is the definition of trouble "said Robert". I know but she was so persistent and wouldn't take no for an answer "Debra replied". Well y'all enjoy yourself "said Robert". I'll try my best RJ "said Debra". The phone rings, hello "answered Debra". Hey girl I know I'm early but I'm outside "shouted Sherry". Well get off the phone and come in "said Debra". I'm out Debby see you when I see you girl "said Robert". Sherry walks in and speaks hi RJ. By CiCi "he replied". Hey Debby! Why RJ leave so quick for "asked Sherry"? Oh RJ got Morgan there, so he got his hands full girl "she answered". Anyways, I have our night planned out girl "said Sherry". Oh really "Debra replied". Yes really girl "Sherry added". No crazy stuff CiCi "laughs Debra". What are you talking about Debby "asked Sherry"? You know what I'm talking about girl "she answered". Anyways I have our night planned out no crazy stuff girl "Sherry replied". And where your kids are "asked Debra"? With their crazy father, exactly where they need to be girl "answered Sherry". You're so silly "Debra laughs". Girl I'm telling the truth "Sherry added". Well let me get cleaned up and I'll be ready "Debra shouted". Ok girl I'll be right here "Sherry replied". Debra goes in the other room to get cleaned up.

CHAPTER THREE

They arrive at a very nice club playing love songs and oldies. Thing girl it is so packed in here "Debra shouted". I know isn't that cool girl "Sherry replied". No silly I can't move around or even here myself "said Debra". Oh girls stop whining and party "Sherry shouted". I'm having a seat in the back CiCi "Debra replied". Ok girl "Sherry shouted".

Debra found a vacant table in the back. She sat down at the table and stared at the crowd but her mind was still on her daughter Morgan and her deceased husband. Then a clean cut fellow walks up to her table. Hi I'm Allen may I sit here "he asked"? I guess you can "Debra replied". So what is your name "he asked"? Look mister I just lost my husband in Iraq "she answered". I'm sorry I lost my wife to a drunk driver "he replied". Oh I'm so sorry, my name is Debra "she replied". James was my world and the father of my only child "said Debra". I had two kids "said Allen. You had "asked Debra". Yeah they were in the car with my wife "Allen replied". I'm so sorry Allen "she added. My pastor been counseling me so I'm making it "said Allen". Oh my God I couldn't make it without my daughter Morgan "replied Debra". I know no one could fill James shoes but will you take my number "said Allen". Yes, yes I will "she replied". Man I can't believe I'm here in a club "said Allen". You, I let my crazy cousin drag me here "laughs Debra". Really, I let my coworkers drag me here "replied Allen". Well we got something in common "laughs Debra". Yeah we do don't we, Debra let me buy you a drink "said Allen". Well I was just about to leave "she replied". Come one sweetie, you deserve it "he said". Ok Allen maybe one "she replied". They ordered their drinks and when there drinks arrive they began to chat. So what did James do before enlisting in the service "asked Allen"? Oh James played college basket ball until I got pregnant "Debra answered". Really, I played division 2 for Arkansas tech "he replied". Really that's crazy "said Debra". Yeah I know right "said Allen". James played for the Miami Hurricanes "said Debra". Man that's awesome "he replied". Yeah he was "she added". Well I must leave because of an early work day so call me some time said Allen, then he gave her a business card. Thanks Allen I'm also leaving "she replied". So can I give you a ride "asked Allen"? No I'm ok but thanks anyway "she replied". Are you sure "he asked"? Yes I'm sure "she laughs". Well I offered "he also laughs". I got to find my cousin and tell her I'm leaving bye Allen "said Debra". Hope to hear from you Debra "he replied". They went their separate ways that night feeling different that they met and hope to maybe one across the other hopefully in the future.

The next day on a pretty Saturday morning Sherry wakes up at Debra's house with a hangover. My head is killing me girl "yelled Sherry". You should be use to it by now "laughs Debra". Did I get laid last night Debby "said Sherry". No CiCi "laughs Debra". Are you sure girl "asked Sherry"? I positive silly "Debra said". Anyways who was that guy you talking to at the club "asked Sherry"? His name is Allen and he's no one "said Debra". Could've fooled me girl, I saw you take his number "yelled Sherry". Well he seemed cool "Debra replied". Don't forget you met him in a club girl "said Sherry". Girl look who's talking "replied Debra". What are you talking about Debby "asked Sherry"? Never mind CiCi "Debra laughs". Robert walks in hey Debby "he spoke". CiCi your baby dad has been calling all night "he added". Hey RJ, my baby dad we'll be fine "said Sherry". Hey RJ "said Debra". Y'all have a good time "asked RJ"? You know I did "Sherry shouted". It was ok "Debra added". Debby was man hunting "said Sherry". I was not "Debra replied". What about Allen "asked Sherry"? Whose Allen "Robert asked"? Allen is no one "Debra replied". You took his number "Sherry added". So "Debra replied". You took who number "asked Robert"? She took Allen number "said Sherry". Debby "Robert shouted"! It was nothing RJ "Debra replied". Yeah right "Sherry added". Look who's talking "laughs Debra". What are you talking about girl "asked Sherry"? Anyways you better be careful sis "said Robert". I will RJ "said Debra". And don't let CiCi get you in any trouble "Robert added". What "asked Sherry"? Never mind CiCi "said Robert". I'll be fine RJ "Debra replied". Well I got to go back to the evil kids I'll talk to y'all later "said Robert". Bye RJ, I love you "said Debra" bye Debby I love you too "he replied". Love you too RJ "Sherry shouted". Bye CiCi "said Robert", then he left. That boy is right, girl you need to slow down "said Sherry". Oh girl I know you didn't just go there "said Debra". I'm about to go tame my man and the kids I'll talk to you later Debby "said Sherry". Bye CiCi, you take care of yourself "said Debra". Oh I will, call me later girl "said Sherry". I will "say Debra". Sherry leaves and Debra lay back down.

CHAPTER FOUR

Two months went by and Debra runs across the business card she got from Allen. Now she's pacing thinking about calling the number. Finally she goes through and makes the call. The phone rang three times and she was going to hang up but a man answers. Hello I'm Debra; I got your number from the club a few months back "she said nervously". Oh hi how are you "he responded with excitement in his voice"? I'm fine and you "she replied"? Much better now that you called "said Allen". How about a dinner so we can catch up, my treat "he added"? Ok that sounds nice "she replied". How about Italian "he asked"? Ok that sounds nice "she answered". So what do you do for a living "he asked"? I'm a social worker and you "she replied". Oh I own Pesto's Italian Diner down town "he answered". Really, that's nice "she added". Yeah but business been slow "he said with concern on his voice". With the right promotion it'll get better I promise "she said to him". Moments later Robert walks in. hey Debby "said Robert". Who's that "asked Allen"? Oh that's my baby brother RJ "she answered". Who you on the phone with "asked Robert"? That better not be CiCi "said Robert". No RJ, it's my friend Allen "she replied".

Hoping to be more "said Allen". You mean the guy from the club "asked Robert"? Yes RJ "shouted Debra". He sounds concern "said Allen". Yeah that's how he is "she replied". Debby where is CiCi "asked Robert"? Her man has been calling me all day long "added Robert". I don't know RJ "she replied". Did you call her cell phone "asked Debra"? No I haven't "said Robert". I'll call you back Allen, because I must find my cousin "said Debra". Ok I'll pick you up at 8:30 tonight sweetie "said Allen". Sounds like a plan "she replied". Well I'll talk to you then "Allen added". Ok talk to you later "she replied" then she hung up. The phone rang and Debra answer "hello". Hi I'm a nurse at the state hospital "the lady on the phone replied". Is this Debra Jones the "nurse added"? Yes it is what's wrong "asked Debra"? We have your cousin Sherry Washington is here "said the nurse". What's wrong "asked Debra"? She's been raped and beaten "said the nurse". Oh my God "screamed Debby". What's wrong "asked Robert"? It's CiCi we got to go to the hospital "Debra shouted". She hangs up the phone and they had to the hospital.

Debra and Robert make it to the hospital and quietly sneak in Sherry's room. Hey RJ, Debby is that y'all "asked Sherry"? Yeah, baby it's us "replied Debra". CiCi I'm going to kill whoever did this to you "said Robert". Thanks RJ but God got it "Sherry replied". I'm sorry CiCi that I wasn't there to protect you "cried Debra". Ah girl it wasn't your fault "said Sherry". I want to find out who did this to you "shouted Robert". Some drunk in the club "she replied". Do you need anything Sherry "asked Debra"? Oh I'm fine, I have booze under the bed "laughs Sherry". Same old CiCi "laughs Robert". No you didn't girl "said Debra". Oh yeah I need it girl "said Sherry". Well I'll stay and take care of you "said Robert". Oh no my baby dad will be home soon

"Sherry laughs". You know I'll stay girl "said Debra". Debby you my girl but I'm cool "shouted Sherry". Are you sure girl "asked Robert"? Yeah RJ I'm cool, I love you guys "said Sherry". I love you too but if you tell anybody else I'll have to kill you "said Robert". Well I got tonight with Allen "said Debra". Be careful girl because he was clubbing "said Sherry". I'll be alright "said Debra". So when do I meet this Allen "asked Robert"? I got to get to know him first RJ "Debra answered". I'm just saying Debby "said Robert". Yeah Debby we meet him "Sherry added". You need to rest CiCi and Robert it's just a date "said Debra". CiCi said the same thing and came home with three kids "said Robert". You wrong for that RJ "Sherry replied". Sure is "laughs Debra". What isn't that how it happen "asked Robert"? Boy you are so silly "laughs Debra". Y'all know it's the truth "said Robert". You all ways picking on me RJ "said Sherry". That's why I'm here sweetie "replied Robert". Y'all always have my back "said Sherry". We are family girl "said Debra". Only by blood "Robert replied". Anyways I love y'all so much "said Sherry". We love you too CiCi "said Debra". Yeah we family "said Robert". I know and I just want to thank you two for everything "said Sherry". A nurse walks in, ok we have more tests to do but you guys can come back later. Ok by CiCi we love you "said Debra". Yeah CiCi we love you and take care of yourself "Robert added"? I know y'all do and I love y'all too "replied Sherry". They hug then Debra and Robert left.

Boy why are you telling people my business "laugh Debra"? You are my business sis so your business is mined as well "he replied. They laugh the whole way home.

CHAPTER FIVE

Later Debra went to her mother house. Hey Debby did you see Sherry "her mother asked"? Yeah mother me and RJ checked on her "Debra answered". How is she doing sugar "asked her mother"? You know CiCi is a fighter momma "Debra replied". I'm going to have the church to pray for her Sunday "added her mother". That's good mother she truly need it "said Debra". Oh we all need it baby "said her mother". First James get killed now CiCi gets raped momma what's next "cried Debra". Her mother hugs her as Debra began to cry her heart out. There, there Debby the Lord allows these trials to prepare for the journeys ahead "her mother said". Well I don't need any more momma I really don't "cried Debra". That's for God to decide Debby "said her mother". I know mother "replied Debra". That's right just keep God first so you will be prepared for that journey he is preparing for you "her mother replied". You're so right momma "said Debra". So if you want to help Sherry then pray for her and let God work, I know its hard baby believe "her mother added". Morgan comes in the room. Hey mommy and grandma "said Morgan". Hi sugar "her grandma replied". Hi baby how's school "asked Debra"? It was ok momma "answered Morgan. Then Morgan ran outside to play. Now Sherry told me about that little boyfriend of yours Debby "said her mother". He is not my boyfriend momma "said Debra". Uh hum that what Sherry said then she came home with three kids "her mother laughs". Now momma you are so wrong for that "Debra laughs". So when do I meet this young fellow Debby "her mother asked"? Can I get to know the boy first momma "Debra laughs"? Well can I at least know who's handling my daughter "her mother replied". Mom "screamed Debra". I'm serious Debby "said her mother". Yes ma'am "said Debra". And where that brother of yours "her mother asked"? Probably at my house taking stuff as usual "Debra laughs". I'm going to see Sherry later but I want you to get some rest Debby "her mother said with concern in her voice". Ok mommas tell her I love her so much "said Debra". I will child now gone and get some rest "her mother added". Ok mother, Morgan lets go "said Debra". No let that child alone she's fine "her mother replied". You sure mother "asked Debra"? Yes child now let us alone child "her mother laughs". Thanks mother I love you so much "replied Debra". They hug each other then Debra kissed Morgan and left.

That Friday Debra and Allen met up at a well respected Italian restaurant. You look very nice Debra "said Allen". Thanks but call me Debby "Debra replied". Ok well you look nice Debby "laughs Allen". So do you Allen "she replied". So how life is after James "asked Allen"? Well where do I start "she laughs"? My cousin gets beat and rape while Morgan still isn't over her dad and it's affecting he school work "she added". Are you over her father "asked Allen"? Well you kind of put me on the spot Allen "she replied". I'm sorry just trying to understand "said Allen". No you're fine it's just that James was my everything "she replied". I understand, my wife and kids is what I base my life around "said Allen". And

I still dream of them like they never left "he added". I mean James was far from perfect but he was perfect to me "said Debra". So tell me what do you like most in a man Debby "asked Allen"? Honesty, loyalty, supportive, loves me for me, and accepts my daughter "she answered". I think you're something special Debby I really do "said Allen". Thanks but I'm just Mrs. Jones little girl "she replied". Yeah but there's something about you sweetie "he added". Ok what do you like in a woman "laughs Debra"? Well fun, attractive, loves life, smart, and someone who loves me for me, "Allen answered". I' just a simple girl that's very easy to please "said Debra". And maybe I can be that simple guy that steals your heart "he replied". You have to meet my daughter Morgan; she is a character and so funny "said Debra". I'm looking forward to one day meeting her "he replied". So what do you do on your spare time "asked Debra?" I work out a little and often try to travel as much as possible "he answered". What was your wife like "asked Debra"? She was funny, always laughing and playing with the kids "he answered". Do you have any family around here left "she asked"? No all of my family is from Michigan "Allen answered". Oh really what part are you from "she asked with aw on her face"? Oh I'm from Flint but lived a year in Detroit "he answered". So do you ever visit them any "asked Debra"? Of course but only on major holidays such as Christmas and Thanksgiving "he answered". Really! I couldn't imagine that amount of time away from RJ and my mother "said Debra". Ok RJ is your little brother right "asked Allen"? Yeah he's my momma's baby boy with his worrisome self "laughs Debra". I bet he's very protective of you to Debby "said Allen". Yes he is just like his father "laughs Debra". So how is your mother doing "asked Allen?" She's old fashion and very faithful to God and the church "said Debra". My parents run a church back home while my big brother preaches in it "said Allen".

Really, that's nice "Debra says with a big smile on her face". Yes Debby I was raised with a heavy Christian back ground "said Allen". Well honey it's getting late and I must get you home "he added". Well I guess you are right Allen, time flies when you're having fun "she replied". So you're having fun "Allen laughs". Yeah it has been fun and I hope to do this again some time "said Debra". Allen waves at his waitress to get her attention and when the young lady came over he asked for the check. He paid the check and walked to the car.

Allen turned on the local R&B station as he drove out the parking lot of the restaurant. So do you like it here "ask Debra trying to break the silence in the car"? Yeah it sort of feels like home here "Allen replied". I bet because we are generally family orient here "said Debra". That is so true because no matter where I go around here the people are so generous "said Allen.

Allen finally pulls up in front of Debra's house. So do you want me to walk you inside Debby "asks Allen"? Sure I don't see any harm in that "she replied". Allen walks her to the front door as she scramble around in her purse to find her house keys. She finds her keys and began to unlock her front door as Allen grabs her waist. Well I'm about to go home but you have my number Debby "said Allen". He stares her in the eyes for about 15 seconds then laid a big kiss on her. She was shocked but didn't stop it. She knew it was sudden but it felt so right she thought. This is too soon "said Debby". I know baby but I feel so comfortable with you "he whispered". She opened the door and went inside but Allen followed while kissing her. They were in the living room kissing like two horny teen agers. Now they're in the kitchen where Allen lifts Debra on the counter and continue to kiss her like a couple that been away from each other for a long time. He lifts his hand up her shirt pulling her breasts out of her bra. She climbed off of the counter pulling his shirt over his head. He took her pulled her shirt off and stared for a moment then said "you don't have to do this Debby. I know but I do want to Allen "she replied". He began to kiss her again and slowly started going down on her and when he got to her belly button he slowly took off her pants and panties and began giving her oral sex. She started moaning of sweet pleasure. Moments later she had her first orgasm since her ex husband past and it was a feeling she missed and enjoyed. She then pulled Allen up from beneath her thighs and pushed him on his back, pulled his pants off slowly and began giving him the best oral sex that he ever had and it wasn't long before he had an orgasm but he was still hard like he just started. Debra stood up and grabs Allen hand to lead him to the bed room. And when they made it to the bed room they proceed to have long passionate sex like it was their last time seeing each other. The air was filled with the lovely smell of making love.

CHAPTER SIX

The next morning Allen wakes up to the smell of bacon and eggs. Here go some breakfast "said Debra" as she approach the bed room. Thanks Debby "he replied". He ate his breakfast and notice Debra staring at him. Are you ok "asked Allen"? Sure Allen it just been a minute "she answered". After he finished his breakfast he got dressed because he had to go to work. Debra walked him to the door and watched him get in the car. As Allen pulled out of the drive way Robert pulls up.

Debby I seen a car leaving here who was that "he asked"? That was Allen, RJ "she replied". Did he spend a night here "he asked"? Yeah RJ now mined your own business "said Debra". News flash Debby, you are my business "said Robert". I am a grown woman and fully capable of taking care of me "said Debra". I'm going to tell mom "said Robert". You wouldn't dare "replied Debra". Try me sis "said Robert". Fine RJ what do you want from me "she asked"? I want to meet this guy of yours "he answered". Ok RJ I'll bring him as soon as possible "she replied". You better Debby, I'm serious sis "added Robert". Anyways how's CiCi "asked Debra"? Oh she's home now Debby, let's go see her "shouted

23

Robert in excitement". Sure that will be nice "replied Debra". Robert stumbles across a wallet. Who wallet is this girl "asked Robert"? Oh my God he left his wallet and we must take it to him at his job "said Debby"! Oh good I'm going to "said Robert". RJ "screamed Debra". What, I need want to meet this guy of yours "said Robert". Ok RJ we'll take Allen his wallet then head strait to CiCi's "said Debra". Oh I got to tell CiCi about this Allen fellow "said Robert". Well I guess it's better than telling mom "said Debra". Well Debby mom is bound to find out "said Robert". I'll tell her when the time is right "said Debra". Yeah you better before she finds out from someone else "said Robert". Anyways I'm just trying to find a good man RJ "said Debra". Well Miss Thing, you don't find one in the club "said Robert". Come on crazy boy, lets go "said Debra". Ok "laughs Robert". They get in the car and heads to Allen job.

They make it to Allen job. Ok RJ I'm going inside to give him his wallet I'll be right back "said Debra". Yeah right sis I'm coming with you "Robert replied". Ok fine RJ "said Debra". They both go inside and approach Allen. Allen spots them and smiles. Hey Allen, here you left your wallet "said Debra". Oh where's my manners this is my brother RJ, and RJ meet Allen "said Debra as she introduce the two". Hi Robert "said Allen". Oh hi dude "replied Robert". We were actually on our way to see my cousin CiCi "said Debra". Well let me at least whip you guys something quick to eat "said Allen". Nah I'm ok "said Robert". Yeah we better get going and meet my cousin CiCi "said Debra". Well at least take home some drinks "said Allen". Nah I'm ok "replied Robert". Yeah sweetie we really must get going "said Debra". So are you dating my sister "asked Robert"? RJ "screamed Debra"! No it's fine Debby "said Allen". Yes sir we are dating but I hope to be much more "added Allen". Oh I had to ask man because Debby never tells us anything

"said Robert". So Allen who is your people "asked Robert".
0h my families are from Michigan "Allen answered". Stop it
RJ that's enough from you "screamed Debra". Do you have
any baby mammas "asked Robert"? I was married but my
wife and kids have passed "said Allen". I'm sorry about him
Allen he is just like his father "said Debra". He was your
father too Debby "said Robert". Allen I'm sorry for this I
was supposed to just drop off your wallet "Debra added".
Don't be honey he's just being a brother so I completely
understands "said Allen". Well I'll call you later Allen "said
Debra". Ok Debby I'll be waiting on your call "replied
Allen". Later Robert and it was nice to meet you "Allen
added". Alright Mr. Allen "said Robert". Debra kissed Allen
then her and Robert left.

Later they arrive at Sherry's house. They walk into the
home like it was their own place. Hi CiCi how are you
"asked Debra"? Hey Debby and RJ, I can't believe you made
it "said Sherry". Hey CiCi yeah we made it "said Robert".
How you are girl "asked Debby"? Girl I'm ok still stunned
a little though "said Sherry". I know something that'll cheer
you up CiCi "said Robert" with an evil little smile on his
face. You better not RJ "said Debra". Oh but it's too good
to keep from CiCi "said Robert". What y'all keeping from
me "asked Sherry"? Debby let that Allen dude spend a night
at her house "Robert screamed"! I can't believe you said
that RJ "said Debra". Oh my God Sherry, you know better
than that "said Sherry". Yeah girl I know "said Robert". It
was nothing "said Debra". Oh it was something for you
to let that man spend a night "replied Sherry". I don't like
him because he gives off a sneaky vibe "said Robert". Boy
you are crazy and don't approve any one that I date "said
Debra". Nah Debby I'm serious and he is hiding something
"said Robert". So when do I meet this fellow "asked Sherry"?
Whenever he leaves his wallet again "said Robert". That's

enough RJ "said Debby". Oh is it Debby "said Robert". Your brother might be right Debby "said Sherry". Enough about me we came to visit you Sherry "said Debra". I'm fine but now I'm worried about you "said Sherry". Yeah CiCi I want names on your violators "said Robert". I told the police RJ so let them do their job "Sherry replied". When it comes to family CiCi I am the police "said Robert". Yeah you're right about that "Debra laughs". Now what is that suppose to mean Debby "asked Robert"? Anyways CiCi do you need anything "asked Debra"? Yeah, I need to meet this guy of yours girl "shouted Sherry"! Same old CiCi "laughs Debra". Whenever momma meets this dude she going to tell you the same thing I've been telling you "said Robert". You better think this through Debby "Sherry added". I will you guys, I promise "said Debra". Don't get off the subject CiCi I still want names of your attacker "said Robert". Let it alone RJ the police will handle it boy "Sherry shouted". The police are not protecting and serving so I'll do the job they can't or won't "say Robert". Boy did Momma Jones drop you on your big head or something "Sherry laughs". Twice "Debra added". What are you to talking about, I'm just being me "said Robert". Yeah that's exactly what I'm talking about boy, anyways Debby bring him to church sometime "said Sherry". CiCi you will meet him soon now stop it "says Debra in a tone of aggravation". Like I said he will have to leave another wallet "said Robert". Anyways girl we are about to leave so just give us a call if you need anything sweetie "said Debra". I will girl, y'all take care and I love y'all "said Sherry". We love you too CiCi "said Debra". Yeah, yeah "Robert added". Ok I need a hug and yes that include you too RJ "said Sherry". They both hug Sherry then got in the car an

CHAPTER SEVEN

Three weeks has gone by since Allen and Debby started dating and Debby has been trying to break the news to her family. She believes she's in love and must find a way to tell her mother. She also doesn't want her family judging her.

On a very sunny but pretty Friday Debby woke up at Allen's house. So what do you think of the place Debby "asked Allen"? Oh I love your place Allen; it's a very beautiful place honey "Debra answered". Now I know it's not much but its home to me "Allen laughs". Its gorgeous baby "said Debra". You know we have been dating for about a month Allen and you still haven't met my mother "said Debra". I'm sorry baby, business has been picking up but we will stop over there together tomorrow afternoon "said Allen". Are you serious Allen "asked Debra with excitement in her voice"? Of course I'm serious Debby; I would do anything to make you happy "replied Allen". Man baby that was easier than I thought "said Debra". Well it's about time you move in with me Debby "said Allen". Oh Allen I couldn't do that "said Debra". Why not honey, don't you have feelings for me "asked Allen"? My feelings are strong for you Allen but I own my house and its Morgan's home "replied Debra". Well Debby you can make this home "Allen replied". I really don't know about all of this, it is so sudden "said Debra". Ok I tell you what honey, you pray on it then make your decision "said Allen". Ok honey I sure will "said Debra". So you say your mother don't know about me "said Allen". No she doesn't, but then again RJ is my little brother "laughs Debra". So does your brother RJ even likes me "asked Allen"? Baby you know RJ is just RJ "said Debra". But does he like me Debby "asked Allen". Debra took a long pause. I completely understand if he doesn't Debby "said Allen". Baby RJ just thinks you are hiding something "said Debra". You guys are close so I must earn his trust Debby "said Allen with concern in his voice". He'll come around Allen I promise he will "said Debra". Debby will you be my wife "asked Allen"? What are you talking about Allen "laughs Debra"? I'm serious Debby I want you to marry me "added Allen. But this is so sudden don't you think honey "asked Debra"? I know but I love you and want you to take this ring "said Allen as he got on one knee taking a ring out of his pocket". But Allen "Debra replied while getting emotional and shedding a tear". Save your words baby and at least think about it "said Allen". Then he kissed her and they made passionate love throughout the night. They wake up around 4:00am but just lay in bed and talk. Ok Allen I'll move in but let me think about this marriage thing sweetie "said Debra". Thanks babe I love you so much "said Allen". You are very welcome and I love you too "Debra replied".

Later that day the couple visited Debra's family at her mother's house. Hello mother, this Allen and Allen this is my mother "said Debra". Hi Allen it is nice to meet you "said mother". Sherry comes from the kitchen to greet the couple. Hi there I'm Sherry or CiCi "said a very jittery Sherry". It is nice to meet you I'm Allen "he replied". Robert enters the room. What's up "greeted Robert"? Nothing much just meeting your family man "Allen replied". Hello RJ "said Debra". Hi sis, Morgan is outside playing "Robert replied". Oh I'll go get her "said Debra with excitement in her voice". So who are your folks "asked Mother Jones"? My family is from Michigan ma'am "Allen answered". What brings you down this way "asked Robert"? The warm weather, nah I'm just kidding I let my deceased wife vision of the south get me here "replied Allen". So was she from here "asked Robert"? Before he could answer Debra entered the room with her daughter Morgan. Hey Allen this is my precious daughter Morgan "said an excited Debra". Hi Morgan I'm Allen "he greeted". Hello mister I'm Morgan "she replied". No sweetie you can call me Allen "he laugh". Do you have any friends I can have "asked Sherry"? Oh baby please don't pay my crazy cousin any mind "laugh Debra". I want to marry your daughter Mrs. Jones "said Allen". The whole house gets quiet. Umm excuse me young man, you what "asked Mother Jones". I'm so sorry but I'm in love with Debby and would love your blessings "Allen replied". A little too soon for that isn't dude "said Robert". Believe me brother your sister is in great hands "said Allen". You need to watch yourself fool "said Robert. Look I don't want or need any trouble "Allen replied". So have you even thought to pray on it baby "asked Mother Jones". No mother I didn't but you know I will "say Debra". Y'all need to come to church this Sunday so we all can pray on it Debby "Sherry added". No because I'm moving Sunday and will be busy all weekend "Debra replied". What "screamed Robert"? So you are moving out of our father's house "asked Robert with sadness to his voice"? Yes I am RJ, now I know it is sudden but it feels right "shouted Debra". Honey your feelings will deceive you some time "added Mother Jones". Yeah like premarital sex "Sherry added". Forget all of that sis, where are you moving too "Robert asked"? I'm moving in with

Allen "Debra replied". Mother is right sis maybe you should pray on it "said Robert". Man Debby you move fast "laughs Sherry". Well we're leaving, are you coming Morgan "asked Debra"? I'm going to hang up with grandmother if it's ok mother "Morgan replied". Ok baby I love you "said Debra then she kissed Morgan on top of her head". I love you too momma "said Morgan then she ran off to play". I love you guys and I'm gone "said Debra as she was leaving". Well it was nice meeting you guys "said Allen as he followed Debra out the door". There something about that boy I seriously don't like "said Mother Jones". I knew you would feel that way mother "said Robert".

CHAPTER EIGHT

Two months has gone by since Debra introduced Allen to her family. Baby I'm about to go visit CiCi are you coming "asked Debra"? No honey why are you visiting CiCi all of a sudden "Allen asked"? Nothing special honey I just haven't seen or heard from her in a while "Debra replied". You mean the cousin that clubs and party 24/7 "Allen added". Baby you are more than welcome to come "said Debra". Nah I'm fine right here, but I'll be waiting on you Debby "said Allen". So when do I meet your family Allen "asked Debra"? Soon Debra "he replied in an angered way". What's your problem Allen "asked Debra"? I'm fine "he replied". You talk about marriage and I don't even know your family "she added". Debby you know my family is up north so don't start with me today "said Allen". Yeah but we have multiple cars so don't give me that lame excuse "she replied". I also have a business to run honey "said Allen in an aggravated tone". Sure I know and understand that but you hired managers for that Allen "said Debra". We will visit my family soon Debby now just drop it "yelled Allen". Yeah probably years from now after we have walking kids "Debra laughs". What was that woman "screamed Allen"? Excuse me but my name is Debra not woman "Debra shouted". You heard what I said Debby and I mean what I say "shouted Allen". What is wrong with you Allen, you use to be so sweet "cried Debra". Nothing is wrong with me Debby maybe it's all you for once woman "he replied". I don't want to fight with you Allen so please talk to me about it "Debra cried". Ok I agree so stop auguring with me Debby "Allen shouted". I am not and you are crazy so maybe I'll just leave "said Debra". Allen storms over to Debra grab her then he slapped her so hard that she fell to the ground. Shut up Debby now look what you made me do "he screamed". Debra starts to cry more in shock than in pain. What is wrong with you Allen "she cried"? I'm so sorry Debby I guess I kind of blacked out because I really don't remember a thing honey "Allen cried". You hit me in the face Allen, you really hit me in the face and I'm afraid of you honey "cried Debra". Allen began to cry so hard as if he was in pain or even assaulted. I'm so sorry and I'll just leave you because you deserve so much better "cried Allen". No baby we will work through it and it will get better "said Debra with still tears flowing down her face". Ok baby maybe you are right and I love you so much for staying with me "he cried". I'll stay with you tonight and maybe see CiCi some other time "said Debra". Are you sure baby "asked Allen"? Yes baby I'm sure "said Debra as she pull Allen toward her and held him with his head on her bussom". Thanks baby I love you so much for just being there for me "said Allen". They held each other for the rest of the night.

Robert walks in Sherry home like he owns the place. Hi RJ what are you doing here "Sherry asked"? I need you to help me look up Allen Ford background to see who this guy is "Robert answered". Are you serious RJ, why and what's wrong "asked Sherry"? I don't know him and he keeps Debby away from us like she don't have family or something "said Robert with concern on his face". That is so true and I haven't seen Debby in about two months "Sherry replied". We don't know him or his people but he knows all about our people CiCi "said Robert". That is true also and he has this tuff guy present over his smooth cut look "said Sherry". CiCi I really think this fool is hiding a crazy secret from us "said Robert". Infact he always has an excuse in not telling us who his people are and I know there's a reason behind it "Robert added". Alright CiCi and RJ in action once again "screamed Sherry". Calm down crazy girl "laughs Robert", and you are right now let's get to business "he added". I wander was his so call restaurant family funded "said Sherry". I don't know but we shall find out CiCi "Robert replied". It's my entire fault for taking her clubbing "said Sherry". I mean she wouldn't have ever met that man if it wasn't for me RJ "cried Sherry". Nah CiCi it wasn't your fault because my sis is a grown woman "replied Robert". I bet Momma Jones is so worried about her "said Sherry". Yeah but she hides it well "Robert replied". Ok RJ lets go to Debby's after this background check come back "Sherry added". Sounds like a plan CiCi, Debby will be so surprised to see us "said Robert". You know what RJ "said Sherry". What "he asked"? Ok, what if this Allen is a killer or something RJ "asked Sherry"? That will be so scary CiCi "he answered". I know but what if RJ "she asked". Then we better get to work CiCi and fast "said Robert". Roger that RJ "said Sherry". The two went on the computer to look up Allen Ford and even had the police to do a background check preparing for the worst but hoping for the best.

That night after Allen fell asleep Debra laid there wandering did she make a mistake. She has never been through a domestic case before with her deceased husband James. She decided to stay strong and work through her situation with Allen. Before she went back to sleep she prayed for knowledge, wisdom, and strength then she fell asleep.

CHAPTER NINE

A month went by and Allen and Debra have been working on their relationship. Debra prepared a meal for her and Allen. Hey baby do you like your dinner honey "Debra asked"? Not at all girl, this taste like crap "Allen yelled". Allen what's wrong with you and why are you're being so mean to me "asked Debra with tears in her eyes"? Just shut up and stop your wining "said Allen". Then he through his food all over the floor screaming "shut up and clean up this mess you just made". No Allen you clean up your own mess and I'm leaving you for real this time "Debra shouted". Look women I said clean up this mess and I won't tell you again "screamed Allen". Allen you are crazy and I'm not going to live here with you anymore "cried Debra". Allen stops screaming and began to laugh. So I'm crazy huh "he laugh". Yes you are and I am leaving you because I don't deserve this from you Allen "Debra replied". Debra grabbed some clothes and began to leave. If you walk one more step near that door I will kill you where you stand Debby "said Allen in a quiet but evil tone". Who are you "asked Debra"? The one you do not want to mess with Debby "he replied". No I won't let you bully me like this anymore Allen Ford "she shouted". And God knows I really don't deserve your mess "she added". Oh ok I forgot that you are the new queen of England "he laughs in an evil sneaky way". You're crazy and I'm going to my mother's house "she cried". As she attempted to leave Allen raced over to Debra and punched her in the face. She hit the ground and Allen got on top of her slapping her repeatedly. She was crying and screaming "stop Allen stop". He didn't pay her any mine and continue to slap her. Shut up Debby before I kill you in here "he screamed". She scratched Allen in the eyes then pushed him off of her and ran toward the door. Allen quickly got to his feet and grabs her by the hair then pulls her to the bed room laughing and mocking her. What are you planning to do to me "she cried"? You will see princes, that's right Miss Queen of England "he laugh". She starts to resists and fights back with little affect on the over the edge derange man that she once loved. He slaps her twice then pushes her to the bed and began to take her clothes off. She resists and fights back punching and scratching him, again with little or no affect at all. He stares her in the face and began to laugh as if he heard the funniest joke ever told to him. Get off of me Allen you are crazy and I'm done with you "screamed Debra". Nah you going to give it to me when I want and how I want it Debby "said Allen in an evil tone". No Allen I said get off of me "she screamed". Debra kicked Allen between the legs and when he went down she began to run to the door but he quickly got his self together and ran after her. He punches her and she went out like Tyson after the Buster Douglas fight. He stared at her like she was a piece of meat and began to rape her like an untamed animal surrounded by his domestic alike.

CHAPTER TEN

Later at Mother Jones Morgan asked her grandma where her mother was. I don't know dear but we will find out "replied her grandma". Robert walks in the house. Hello momma "he greeted" and hey Morgan "he added". Hello "RJ his mother replied". Hi Uncle Robert "said Morgan". Robert notices a sad expression on Morgan face and he knew something was wrong. He looked at his mother and told Morgan let me speak to your grandmother for a moment. Ok Uncle Robert "she relied" then she went in the other room to watch television. Momma, have you heard from my sister lately "asked Robert"? No RJ so I know something is wrong "she cried". Momma I just know that Allen character is a no good person and I will get to the bottom of it, even if I have to go to the police "said Robert with concern in his voice". Morgan comes back in the room and hugs her grandmother and shed a tear. Momma I have some work to do "said Robert" then he left.

Meanwhile at Allen's Debra is staring at pictures of her family and shed a tear remembering the good times. Ok Debby I know you think I'm crazy but I'm just protecting my investments "said Allen". What are you saying "she asked"? Well I decided that you will be my wife and have my kids "said Allen". Allen I have a daughter already and I love her very much "said Debra". Yeah but that kid isn't mine so we are starting a new family "he said". This will not work and I really want to see my baby but you want let me "she said".

I'll tell you what I might let you see your child as soon as you become pregnant "he replied". Allen that is stupid and selfish "said Debra". Ok woman you need to watch your tongue before you get hurt "he said with anger in his voice". She dropped her head then said nothing else. And besides I know where your family lay their heads at woman "said Allen". Please leave my family out of this "she replied".

Later that day Robert got a shocking phone call from his detective friend Shawn Robertson. Shawn went to school with Robert and they were best friends from grade school on out. Hello Robert "said Shawn". Oh what's up Shawn, how are you "asked Robert"? Nothing much and I'm fine, but I discovered that Mr. Allen Ford is an exconvict that was convicted for drugs and beating his wife "said Shawn". Oh my God man is you freaking serious "said Robert" with concern in his voice". Yeah bro I am serious as a heart attack "replied Shawn". Ok I guess I will try to get my sister to safety "said Robert". That might be good plan because we've learned that his wife actually died from a wreck do to her break lines being cut and Allen is a potential suspect "Shawn added". Man this is more serious than I could have even imagined "said Robert". Yeah bro that is true and I'm trying to get a warrant for his arrest as soon as possible RJ "said Shawn". Thanks a lot Shawn and I'll keep in touch "said Robert". Anytime RJ and just call me any time bro "Shawn replied". And they both hung up. Robert closed his eyes and began to pray then his phone rang. Hello "Robert answered". Hi boy it's me "Sherry replied". Oh hi CiCi I have some news on Allen Ford so I'm on my way over your house "said Robert. Is everything ok "asked Sherry"? I'll tell you when I get there "said Robert" then he hung up grabbed his keys and left his house headed to Sherry's.

CHAPTER ELEVEN

Robert pulls up at Sherry's house and walk in with a blank facial expression. Hi RJ what's wrong "she asked". Well I found some pretty interesting things on this Allen Ford "said Robert". Oh God is it bad RJ "asked Sherry"? Oh yeah CiCi it's real bad "Robert replied". So what exactly do you got on this guy RJ "asked Sherry"? Well CiCi it turns out that Allen has been to prison for drugs and beating his wife "he answered". Oh my God RJ we must warn Debby before it's too late "said Sherry with excitement in her voice". And according to the police on the case of his wife's death it turns out her wreck was planned "said Robert". What do you mean planned RJ "asked Sherry"? Well CiCi her break lines were cut "said Robert". But wasn't his kids in the car "asked Sherry"? Yes they were and it's a shame that no one has been convicted for this crime yet "Robert replied". Yes it is because not only he killed his wife but his kids "Sherry cried". If he has no remorse for his own wife and kids there is no way he will show any for Debby "Robert replied". So I know we going to ride on this fool RJ "said Sherry". Oh yes we are CiCi and this fool won't know what hit him "said Robert with a smirk on his face". Now if momma finds out she will have a heart attack "said Robert". I know RJ so I won't say a word "Sherry replied". Thanks CiCi "said Robert". Robert I too have some news today "said Sherry". What is it CiCi "asked Robert"? I didn't tell you who raped me because I know how you are RJ "said Sherry". Well you are my big cousin we grew up together and I love you too much to watch you hurt CiCi "said Robert with concern in his voice". I know but the police caught the guy this morning "said Sherry". You know what CiCi, besides my kids and momma you and Debby is all I have "said Robert". Boy stop it you are making me cry "said Sherry". Its true Sherry, you and Debby played with me back in the day "Robert replied". Now RJ you always told on us "laughs Sherry". Only because you and Debby always beat me up "Robert laughs". True but you were sort of a pest RJ "she continue to laugh". That is true now let's get back to business CiCi "said Robert". Ok you know I have Allen and Debra address on my nightstand "Sherry replied". Ok we are going over there and I will make sure the police take another look at his wife's death again so we can be prepared to take caution of this man "said Robert". Ok it sounds like a plan RJ just let me grab my phone and purse and I'll be ready "said Sherry". Sherry grabs her phone, purse, then she and Robert rushed out the door headed for the car.

So Debby where is your God now "asked Allen with an evil grin on his face"? She stares at him tears rolling down her face. I rebuke you in the name of Jesus "she screamed". Yes you are having your little fun now but God will see it my way, because the bible says do not touch his anointed "added Debra". Oh believe me I will have the last laugh Debby so you can keep those bible scriptures to yourself "Allen replied". Oh yes I will pray that the Lord have mercy on you when the Lord make you my footstool "said Debra". Allen began to get angry because she continues to speak of

God and in rage he attacked her knocking her out. As he watched her lay his evil perverted thoughts began to take hold as he raped her for hours as she lay helpless.

CHAPTER TWELVE

Debra wakes up and realizes what Allen has done and decided to confront him on his actions. So you wanted to marry me one moment and the next you decide to rape me Allen "shouted Debra". No baby we made love don't you remember honey "said Allen". No Allen you raped me and there is nothing of rape that says love "she replied". So I guess the marriage is off huh "he replied". Are you nuts Allen, I can't love someone like you "she replied". I've been called a crazy a time or two Debby "laughs Allen". So tell me Allen, did you also beat your wife "Debra asked"? Allen began to laugh so hard that he was in tears of laughter. So did you beat your wife or not Allen "she asked"? Little Debby little Debby did you honestly thought this started with you "he laugh". You are sick and twisted in the head Allen "she replied". Yeah I've also been called that two my love "he laugh". You are not the man I fell in love with and I can't have kids with you or even marry you Allen "said Debra". Oh you will be my wife and we will have kids together because we love each other Debby "he replied". No you are sick and need help "said Debra". Allen stared off with a blank on his face. Debra began to put clothes on then Allen turned to her. Where do you think you are going Debby "he asked"? She ignored him and began to put clothes in a bag. Look woman I won't ask again "he replied". Allen I must leave you because I have a daughter and family that really needs me "she replied". Now Debby you know I can't let you go baby I need you "he replied". Oh so you just going to hold me as a hostage huh "she shouted". No baby you are my property and I own you forever "he laugh". No I'm leaving "she replied" and began to walk off but Allen got to her before she could walk past the bed. Now I said you are my property "Allen said with anger in his voice" then he slapped her to the bed. Ok Allen I'll stay if that's what you want "she cried". Yeah I know you are going to stay because I am your master "he screamed". Now clean up this dirty house and you better have dinner ready when I'm ready to eat "he screamed"! Ok Allen whatever you say "she cried". Yeah that's right you better listen because I still know where your family sleep at night sweetie "he laugh". Allen you just keep my family out of this "said Debra". Oh I will as long as you follow my orders and don't try leaving me "he replied". And you expect me to marry you and have kids with you Allen "she replied". What are your motives for this baby because you are a good man that has things going for you "she asked"? I mean you have cars a successful business in town so what are your motives Allen "she asked"? Well Debby I wasn't always well off, Infact my mother was God fearing but my father was a heroin dealer "he answered". I have brother that played pro foot ball and got cut from the team do to his affiliation with the drug dealers in Michigan "he added". Later my dad decided to start pimping and his hookers were only two daughters yeah you heard right my sisters "said a very disturbed Allen". My father offered me the business and when I said no he punched me in my face because he said I was weak "Allen added". So the next day I went to my father and told him I would take the job if he had other hookers instead of my sisters which I loved dearly, he looked me in my face and said son I'm not going to fire your sisters and punched me in the face again "Allen continued". I knew something was wrong with him but I loved him so much Debby "Allen explained". So what exactly did you do to stop him "Debra asked"? Well I started selling drugs and built a local empire that was way bigger than any pimp's empire and I started killing those pimps but when I got to my father I remember him begging me to spare him so I did "said Allen". I told him thanks for teaching me how to be tuff in this tuff world but now this tuff world is done with you and I killed my father and to this day my mom thinks he ran off but I disposed of his body and no one will ever find him until I tell them which definitely not going to happen "said Allen". So you see Debby I do expect you to marry me and have my kids "he laugh". My family will look for me Allen "cried Debra". Yeah that may be but that RJ better stay out my business or he'll be with my father "laugh Allen". You better stay away from my baby brother "cried Debra". Well he better stay away from me and out of my business "said Allen"

Chapter Thirteen

Allen grabs Debra at the early hours around 2:00am and put her in his Mercedes Bens and drove off. Where are you taking me Allen "cried Debra"? I'm glad you asked but we are going to my summer home in Sacramento California Debby "Allen laugh". Did you know kidnapping is a crime in this country "yelled Debra"? Of course honey that's why you came willingly "he laughs". And I also have a restaurant out there as well babe "he added". You are seriously ill Allen and need professional help "she cried". Oh that maybe but right now I have other plans "he replied". Oh I bet you do and it involves rape and kidnapping "said Debra". Oh you think you are funny don't you, huh "he screamed"? He paused for a moment then started laughing like he was the only one in the car. What is your problem Allen "asked Debra with a face full of tears"? I don't have a problem my love but your family will if I don't get what I want Debby "he answered". Ok well what do you want from me then Allen "she asked"? Well you will marry me and give me kids of my own because I am not going to raise James little brat Debby "Allen said with his teeth clinching together". Well you should know that James little brat is my daughter and will be my only child for a while "she replied". Oh is that right Debby "he laughs". Oh yes Allen and you will not get away with your crimes against me "laughs Debra". Oh so now you are tuff now Debby "asked Allen in a sarcastic way"? No not at all sweetie but I know my God is tougher than you can even imagine and when you mess with his people you will pay so harshly that the ones you hurt will have to pray mercy for you "she replied". Really Debby? "Allen laughs". You should know by now Debby that I have the upper hand on you and your God "he continues". No sweetie you don't and I assure you that he has a plan for you and we will see who gets the last laugh.

Meanwhile a Robert and Sherry stop by Debby and Allen's and notices the house has been abandon. Oh my God RJ where could they be "shouted Sherry". I don't know CiCi but it really don't seem to be a planned trip "replied Robert". The two started to search around the house for clues. I got to notify the police CiCi because something isn't right "added Robert". Your mom is going to be so hurt if we don't find Debby soon "Sherry replied". Robert phone received a text from Debra phone that read (Allen kidnapped me and taking me to California). Oh my CiCi we must head out to Cali but what city "cried Robert".

So what are you doing Debby I thought you were sleep "asked Allen". You thought wrong "she replied". Woman I was trying to be nice to you "he replied". Oh see taking me against my will doesn't seem nice in my book "Debra added". Well in my book the woman does what she is told and you is my woman "he replied". Well I don't want to be with you anymore Allen "said Debra". So you think you're going to quit me girl "screamed Allen". He pulled over to a gas station. Now I'm buying gas and some snacks if you decide to run I'll shoot you dead "said Allen" then he showed Debra his gun to scare her. As soon as Allen left the car she text her brother again and it read (we are headed to Sacramento and please don't reply to any of my texts).

Hey CiCi I got another text from Debby saying she is on her way to Sacramento "shouted Robert". Oh RJ lets go I'm going to call my job and Momma Jones and let her know our where about "said Sherry".

I got you some chips and a coke Debby "said Allen". I'm not hungry "she replied". Ok but we still have a long drive ahead of us "he replied". So you really going to keep me from my daughter huh "said Debra". What do you means Debby "Asked Allen"? I thought we should start our own family "laughs Allen". I have my own family Allen and you can't keep me from them forever "Debra replied".

Ok CiCi I'm ready to go and the police are supposed to get us a trace on Debby's phone "said Robert". I told my man and kids to pray for us to bring Debby home safe "Sherry replied". I know momma is going to be worried but we must go through with this "added Robert". I don't know how I could make it without my big sister "said Robert". I know she's my cousin but felt like my sister because we were all we had RJ "said Sherry". Well let's grab our things CiCi and head out "said Robert "as they proceed to leave a phone rang. Hello "Robert answered". I'm officer Tillman, and according to our lab works Allen did kill his wife "said the officer". And we need the where about of the suspect "asked the officer"? Yes sir there headed to Sacramento but he has my sister against her own will "said Robert". Ok as soon as we get a location on your sister cell phone we will let you know something "the officer replied". They hang up and the two left for California.

You awake "asked Allen"? Of course I can't around you "she replied". Well since you are up unzip my pants and do your business "said Allen". Are you crazy Allen "asked Debra"? Maybe I am a little bit but I'm your boss now do what I tell you to do Debby "he said in an anger tone". Do what you have to Allen because I will not do that "said Debra". Oh you must think you really have an option "he replied". All I'm saying is do what you have to do "shout Debra". Allen then looked at her with anger and starts to unzip his pants and warned her if she doesn't do what he asked he will pull over the car. Debra was very afraid but still refuses. He then pulls the car over and began to beat her but Debra tried to fight back but Allen proves to be overwhelmingly stronger than her. After Allen felt that he had beaten enough he then began to rape her as Debra was in and out of consciousness. After he finish he got back in the driver seat and began to drive again. See that wasn't so bad was it "he laughs". She didn't respond as she stared out the window and watched the trees pass her by in the dark.

CiCi if that dude hurt my sis I will kill him "said Robert". I just hope we can get to her before he can do something to her RJ "cried Sherry". I know there was something weird about that dude the minute I met him "Robert added". I know one thing I will never take her out to a club again "Sherry replied". It's not going to be pretty when I get my hands on this dude when I see him CiCi "said Robert.

Mean while Debra and Allen made it to a town with the entrance sign reading welcome to Salt Lake City. Well baby we are not far from California now "Allen shouted". As soon as the car came to a halt Debra opens the door and ran straight to wooded area. Allen pulls the car over and started screaming and cursing that she better come out of hiding or he will kill her when he finds her. She has never been so scared in her life but she stayed in hiding. Ok you want to be like this and just play games Debby "he shouted". Well let's play "he screamed". What are you going to do Debby, hide out her in the woods all night "he asked"?

Mean while Robert got a phone call from a lady in Michigan claiming to be Allen's sister. Hello I'm Allen sister and I'm calling you to let you know that my brother killed our dad when he was younger and that your sister is in more danger than you my know "said the lady". So can you give me the direct address to Allen's place in Sacramento "asked Allen"? I sure will but please don't tell him you got it from me "she replied". Trust me sweetie I won't "he said". He said the address to Sherry to write down while he was driving and talking on the phone to the lady. How sure are you about this ma'am "Robert asks"? Well sir we have an old Cadillac that my mother use to own in my grandmothers back yard "said the lady". And in that car we found pictures of my dad lifeless body "the lady added". Oh my God ma'am did you notify the cops "ask Robert"? No Mister I just found the pictures two days ago "she replied". I know Allen is your brother but he has my sister against her will and may even kill her if we fail to get to them "said Robert". I know Mister and May God be with you "said the lady and she hung up the phone". Robert put the cell phone and told Sherry what the lady had said. They drove with even more determination than before to reach Debby.

Debby I know you're out here you can't hide forever girl "Allen yelled". Allen heard a noise and quickly ran toward it and discovered it was only a possum. Little that he knew Debby saw him and awaited the opportunity to run. She took off like a professional track star. Get here you stupid broad and Allen raced after her trying to catch her. But Debra took advantage of the dark woods and stop to hide again. She was quiet and Allen began to get frustrated because it was so dark and he couldn't find her. Ok since you want to be that way I'll just go get that daughter of yours you stinking slut "screamed Allen". Debra saw him standing there and grabbed a small log and swung at the back of his head. It was a loud cracking sound that sent him to the ground face down. She then took off running while Allen was lying lifeless.

Sherry drove at night so Robert could sleep. But both of them rarely slept as they run the different scenarios through their minds. As they make it to Salt Lake City sherry notice Allen's car. RJ there goes the car screams "Sherry". Oh my God it is the car "Robert replies". But as they were pulling beside the car a beaten up Debra come screaming out of the woods. Robert and Sherry rushed to her and put her in the car. As they were comforting her other motorist pulls over to help. The police were then notified and the group of people stayed with the trio until the officer arrived. Hello is you people ok "asked the officer"? Yes we are now sir "answered Sherry". I was just kidnapped by my fiancé and he is in the woods unconscious "Debra added". Ok you people get to safety I'm going in the woods to get him "said the officer". Please don't go alone Officer because he is armed "said Debra". Thanks ma'am I'll radio for back up "replied the Officer". In a matter of minutes other officers arrived and they attempt to sweep the area to find that their suspect got away. After long interviews Debra gotten cleaned up and the three headed back home. Debra road in the back seat as the other two talked up front. We will get that bastard sis; I promise "said Robert". Thanks RJ "she replied". Is Morgan ok "asked Debra"? Yes sweetie she is "said Sherry". Thank you guys for saving my life "said Debra". It's our job "Robert replied". The phone rang Robert answered "hello". Hey baby did you find your sister "said mom". Yes we did mother "said Robert". Oh well what happen to Allen "asked mother"? The officers never found him momma "replied Debra". Tell mom it will be ok "said Robert". Tell RJ I heard him and to get y'all back home ASAP "said mom". Ok mom he will and I love you "said Debra". They both hang up and though

Debra was in safe hands they couldn't but wonder, where in the hell did Allen go so quickly.

CHAPTER FOURTEEN

Two months had gone by and the police still didn't have a lead on Allen. Debra moved in with her mother and kept her family close to her because in the back of her head she knew Allen was lurking in the dark waiting on her to slip up. Robert and Sherry worked like amateur detectives working on any leads they had receive from the police.

Robert meets Sherry at a nearby café. Hey CiCi I just learned the officers has no knowledge of the home in Sacramento "Robert whispered". RJ how did you find out "she asked". Well the cops looked into the address and learned it is actually in his cousin's name "he replied". Oh my God RJ this is getting deep "she added". Yeah I know and we must help get this guy off of the streets "said Robert". Ok I also have some news RJ "said Sherry". His sister was shot yesterday in Detroit and now in a comma "she added". Damn CiCi he must know she gave us info about him "Robert replied". Ok we must make sure Debby is safe and never alone at any time "he added". Ok that sounds like a plan RJ "she replied".

Mother Jones picks up Morgan from school. Hey grandma "greeted Morgan". Hi sugar "Momma Jones replied". How was school "she added"? It was ok I guess, I'm just so happy momma is home grandma "Morgan answered". Baby the Lord has a big plan for you and your mother, so some crazy man is not going to stop God's plan sugar "laughs Momma Jones". Thanks for just being there for me grandma "said Morgan". It's my job sweetie "she replied". They laugh, talked, and just remember the good old times as they heads to the mall.

Mean while in Detroit Allen sister starts to come to out of a coma and notice over a dozen detectives. Who are you people "she asks"? We are here to help you ma'am, I'm Captain Wilson and I need to ask you some questions. Ok sir what do you want to know "she asked"? Well first off who shot you up like this "he asked". Does it really matter sir "she asks"? Of course it does ma'am "he answered". Well if that was really the case what will you do to protect me from the guy until he's caught "she replied". Ma'am if you need protection we will provide it but I need your help to catch him "he said". You can't protect me and the girl down south is in grave danger "she added". So are you telling me it was your brother "said the officer"? No I didn't say that unless you can make sure I'm safe "she replied". Ok but withholding info can get you in a lot of trouble and even jail time sweetie "said Officer Wilson". She then burst out in laughter. You really don't get it sir; I would rather withhold info than get murdered "she replied". Ok I tell you what an officer will be with you night and day until we get you in protective custody just help us to help you "he cried". Ok but you better get to that Debra girl because she is in danger "she replied". She then began to give the officer what he needed and the cop kept his word on protection.

Hi guys "said Debra as she greeted Robert and Sherry". Hey girl is you ok "asked Sherry"? Yeah CiCi I'm fine because I know God got me "she replied". Hey Debby "said

Robert". Hi RJ "she replied". Have you heard anything about the case on Allen "asked Robert"? No but I'm not worried about him it's been two months and God brought me too far to take me backwards baby bro "she replied". I know Debby but this guy killed other people sis "he added". What RJ "asked Debra in shock"? Yeah Debby he's right, we been doing research on that man for awhile and didn't give you the information because we knew you would be in even more danger if he knew you had that on him "added Sherry". Maybe you're right but he told me some stories about his dark and evil past "said Debra". Yeah but we even got info from his sister "said Robert". How did you manage that type of info "asks Debra"? Well she called us while you were still being kidnapped sis "he replied". Ok let's get going guys, I'll grab the tab ladies "said Robert". The three hugged each other then left.

Two weeks had gone by and the family decided to have a family get together. There were people there that Debra hasn't seen in years. Hey Debby it's your Uncle Pete, girl I haven't seen you in years. Dang uncle you are loud "said Sherry". Shut up girl you louder than all of us put together "Pete replied". An old man looks like he was at least a hundred years old walk in the room. Oh my God Papa you came "Debra shouted". Yeah sweetie I wouldn't have miss this for the world Debby "he replied". They hugged and Morgan was hanging out with cousins she has never met. There were so many people that you could have mistaken them for a church. So Debby has you heard from that Allen fellow "asked one of the older ladies at the get together"? No Aunt Terry the cops' haven't found him yet "Debby replied". Well they better find him before your crazy cousin June bug does "Pete replied". Uncle Pete I thought June was in jail "said Debby". Robert walks in the room. Hey y'all "said Robert". Everyone replied by saying hi and was hugging him. The day went well and Debby enjoyed the day and hoped it would never end but she knew it had to.

Two weeks later in Detroit Allen sister was out of the hospital. She gave the officers what they want but they really didn't keep their word with protection so she tried to stay low profile. She walked down main streets to avoid getting kidnapped or even killed. But she didn't know that the officers were keeping their word by following her and using her as bate to catch her brother.

Debby meets with Sherry to go out to a movie. Are you ready girl "asks Debra"? Yeah girl I'm ready "shouted Sherry". So what do you want to see CiCi "asks Debby"? I don't know "replied Sherry". The two got in Sherry's car and rode off. So how Morgan and your momma are doing "asked Sherry"? They are ok just trying to adjust to life after Allen "laugh Debra". I know that's right girl "said Sherry". You know CiCi being in that car with Allen all I could do is just pray "said Debra". I honestly thought that I was going to die and never see you guys again "she added". Sherry was beginning to get teary eyed as she drove and heard Debra story about riding with Allen. After the movie the two women decided to go to a local jazz bar to just talk. You know Debby, you and RJ is the best thing to ever happen to me "said Sherry". Thanks CiCi, you were with us so much that I felt like we were more like sisters than cousins "Debra replied". You know Allen sister been released from the hospital and she is back on the streets "said Sherry". God be with her because her brother is very dangerous "replied Debra". I'm praying for that girl too "Sherry added". I have been even more committed to God and planning to marry my man and go to church with your mother Debby "said Sherry". Girl I can't believe the words coming out of your mouth "replied Debra". Yeah I know but God has blessed me so much that I just can't abandon him anymore "said

Sherry". Well I'm so proud of you CiCi "said Debra". Thanks girl but I didn't do it alone "said Sherry". The two talked like they haven't seen one another in years. After they shared testimonies they then went home knowing each other better than they did before.

Mean while in Detroit Allen's sister decided to leave her home at midnight to roam the streets. Before could get two blocks she heard noises but tried to ignore it. She heard it again then she began to sprint like she was running a marathon. The police that were supposed to be following her were in their squad car asleep. She began to run even faster and even started to scream but it was a tough neighborhood that's used to screaming through the night. "BOOM" there was a shot and the bullet got her in shoulder. She screams even more. "PAP PAP POW" all three of the final shots went thru her back and out the front. The officers rushed to her body but when they got to her it was too late. She can only stare at the officers as she fight and gasp for air.

Chapter Fifteen

There loud knocks at Sherry's house. Who is beating my door like they are crazy "she said". It's me CiCi "said Robert". Damn RJ it is two in the morning "shouted Sherry". She then let Robert in the house. He had a stunned look on his face like he had just seen a ghost. What's wrong RJ "asks Sherry"? Allen sister just got shot and killed in Detroit while in protective custody "he replied". Oh Jesus, Allen is behind this isn't he "she ask"? I really think so, and that lady really believed the cops would keep her safe "he said with sadness in his voice". We got to protect our family right now because the officers only out for their own "said Sherry". That is true, so we got to protect Debby by any means "he replied". Ok RJ let's do it "she added".

In Detroit the cops was looking dumb founded not knowing where to turn. Even though Allen is the lead suspect there is still no physical evidence. The streets of Detroit were in total shock. It was like dealing with a ghost. No one was coming forward with any information. It was like a case going cold before it even began.

Robert was doing some plotting of his own. He decided to go to some of Allen's places but he wasn't alone, he recruited his cousin June and them. June is always in trouble and didn't care about jail. Are you ready for this RJ "said June"? Yeah June let's do this "replied Robert". June lit a torch to the house Allen owned. A crowd of fifteen men watch as the flames grew. RJ get out of here this isn't you "said June". We'll take care of all of Allen properties, now we just started a war so you better lay low "June added". Robert agreed and left. June then torched some of Allen businesses. Robert knew Allen will be ready for revenge so he decided to go search for his sister ex boyfriend.

Later at the local elementary Debra was there to pick up Morgan but notice a man entering the building looking suspicious. She blows her horn and the man turns to her. It was Allen and he was there to kidnap Morgan. She got out the car to scream as Morgan walks out of the building. Allen then grabs the girl and while Debra race toward him he pulls out a gun and began to shoot. People start to panic and Allen uses it as a divergent and gets into a black Lincoln continental. Debra gets back in her car to follow the car while calling the police. The chase left from a school zone to the highway. After the police joins the chase and Debra then call her brother. RJ the police is on to Allen but in the chase he has Morgan in the car with him "cried Debra". Oh my God Debby, I'm on my way to his Sacramento home "Robert replied". RJ how far is you "ask Debra"? I'm not in town sis but I flew to California this morning "he replied".

The police follow behind but not aggressively do to a minor being in the car. Debra still in shock about the situation and all she can do is pray. At this time she is riding with a detective as they hope he will run out of gas.

Meanwhile Robert makes to Allen home and entered. He walks in and notices a lot of art in the home. He has a sick feeling about the place as he looks around. He hears noises coming from the back. So he then grabs the nearest thing he can grab which turns out to be an old broom. It's not much but it will have to do he thought. As he got closer the noise got louder. He was the scariest he had ever been in his life.

The officers still wanted to keep the chase close but not aggressive. At this time there are news helicopters flying over the cars reporting the story. Allen knew he couldn't get away; he was just buying time and contemplating on his next move. Sherry and Momma Jones were watching the event from home on TV. They were holding each other crying and praying. Debra could see the car knowing that this man has her baby life in her hand. All she could think what is this man thinking and how God will bring her baby out of this.

The noise is getting louder as he gets closer to the back of the house. I can't believe that I'm in this house in California without a real weapon "Robert thought to himself. The noise steady getting louder as he get closer. Robert is now standing in front of the door where the noise is coming from. He then kicks in the door like he owned the place.

Allen is nearly out of gas and his hostage is young but didn't have that fear in her eyes as he has put in so many people in the streets of Michigan. Hey little girl are you afraid for your life "asks Allen". No because God got me so if I were to die I'll be in heaven with my heavenly father "replied Morgan". You are a brave little girl and that will take you far places "said Allen". You can change too "she replied". No I can't and as soon as I'm out of gas that will be the end of my life "said Allen". But it doesn't have to be this way "she said". I'm afraid it does "he replied".

I wondered what he saying to my little girl "thought Debra". They then notice Allen's car starts to slow down. Ok baby doll it is almost show time "said the officer".

Oh my Momma Jones the car is slowing down "said Sherry". Oh God it is CiCi she replied! They watch on TV but they were nervous like they had been on the scene themselves.

Robert finds a room with four girls tied up and blind folded. He then calls 911 and he was in so much shock that he nearly fainted. He untied the ladies and told them the cops are on their way. And he then called Sherry and told her the news.

The car coasts due to lack of gas and the police follow at a safe distance. Debra keeps her eyes locked on the car and still nervous that her little is in the car with a psychopath. She then closes her eyes and began to pray.

Oh CiCi I hope my Morgan get out of this safe "cried Momma Jones". Me too "Sherry cried".

When the officers finally made it to the scene Robert gave them all the information that he had as he watched the girls get escorted to the cars. One of the ladies walk up to Robert hugged him and thanked him for saving them. No ma'am I can't let you give me the credit "said Robert". The Lord deserves all of your thanks "he added". The lady then smiled and got in the patrol car, and she smiled as the car drove off never letting her eyes off of her hero.

The car is at a complete stop. So I guess I'm a dead man "said Allen". But it doesn't have to be that way "replied Morgan". You are young girl and couldn't comprehend all of the wrong doings I'm responsible for "said Allen". But I hope you know that my God in heaven forgives all "she added". Ok little girl you got to get out of this car because it may get ugly "he replied". The little girl hugged Allen and looked at him with a big smile on her face. She then opens the door and ran toward a sea of policemen.

Robert is on his way home but is listening to the news and began to cry tears of joy when he heard the reporter saying Morgan is free from her kidnapper. He began to smile and to himself say "God is good".

The officers grab the girl and bring her to safety the take her to mother. Hey mom "Morgan says with a big smile on her face". Debra then grabs her little girl and with tears running down their faces and hugs her like it was their last time to see each other.

Allen knew there was no way out and he lit up cigarette while staring at the officers through his rearview mirror. All he could do is watch his life fall apart wishing he could go back in time. He then opens the door and began to get out of the car.

The officers in Detroit couldn't believe that there suspect in a handful of killings is about to be in custody and the officers kept their eyes on the television like they were watching the super bowl.

Allen knew there was no way out and he lit up cigarette while staring at the officers through his rearview mirror. All he could do is watch his life fall apart wishing he could go back in time. He then opens the door and began to get out of the car.

The officers in Detroit couldn't believe that there suspect in a handful of killings is about to be in custody and the officers kept their eyes on the television like they were watching the super bowl. Oh my "said Officer Wilson". They finally got this scumbag "he added".

This day is the craziest in my life "Robert thought to his self as his ride home grew closer". He was so happy about saving the girls lives. He also learned that the girls that he saved have been captive for six days by Allen for ransom money. The girls are all from good families with a lot of money. The officers also retrieved the weapon that he used to kill his sister with.

Now Momma Jones house were now full with friends and family members watching the chase on television. They were all so happy to watch Morgan run from the car to the sea of policemen. Pastor mike says prayers and when he finishes the house erupted in cheers. People were hugging and crying of happiness and hope that this day would end without further tragedy. Sherry hugs Pastor Mike and Momma Jones the thanks God for this day. The phone rang and it is Robert. Hey RJ comes on home "She screamed in happiness". I just got off the plane and I'm about an hour away "he replied". It's been seventeen hours and the standoff is nearly over "said Sherry". I know I'm hearing it on the radio right now "Robert said in excitement". Ok all of us is at your momma house and we'll be waiting on you RJ "she replied". They said their goodbyes then hung up.

Get on the ground and drop your weapon "screamed an armed officer". Allen then looks around in amaze of the surreal scene. He then looks at a helicopter almost in disbelief. Get on the ground and drop your weapon "the officer repeated". Debra closes her eyes to pray then opened them to noticed Allen starring her direction from afar.

Robert drives four miles over the limit in hopes of getting to his family so he can be there to comfort them. He listens to the radio and feels something could go wrong if Allen doesn't drop his gun. All he could do is doing what the rest of America is doing, which is watching this event from the view of the media. He takes a deep sigh and began to pray for this to be over. He then called his wife and told her will be home soon and to meet him at his mother house. They then hang up to see this event unfold.

Allen gives Debra a stare but not an evil one. He then turns to the officers yelling at him. Get your but on the ground and drop the weapon Allen; this will be our last time telling you "screamed the officer". Allen began to shed tears then raise his gun to attempt to fire but the officers' opened fire before he could. The shots sound like a rift of thunder in the midst of the battle of Armageddon. The country watched as Allen bullet riddle body dropped to the ground. He took one last breath before his body gave up and his body lay lifeless in front of America.

Robert finally makes it to town but heard the news on the radio. He then drives like a madman trying to reach his family. Though he doesn't condone violence he knew it had to be God will. He then let off a sigh of relief that this is all over and only one person lost their life instead of more.

Debra began to hold Morgan tight and wept like she had just lost a family member. Then the officers escorted her to her to her car. Momma he talked to me in the car but he wasn't mad "said Morgan". What did he say baby "Debra asked". He just apologized and said he wish he could do it all over again so he could be a better person "she answered". Debra looks at her daughter kiss her on the forehead then starts the car. They drove off headed to the family house.

Robert pulls up in front of his mother house and the family poured out of the house greeting and hugged him. He was so happy to see them all he could do is smile. Forty minutes later Debra pulls up and ran into the crowed of family members.

A week later Debra went to Allen's funeral and she sat in the back of the church. She didn't go to really support him but to do a Godly thing and show up for a man that has no friends. There were less than fifty people there. And when the preacher asks for someone to speak on behave of Allen no one stood up so she did it. She got up there and was speechless. So she took a breath, closed her eyes, and began to pray. Then she opened her eyes and spoke to the small crowed. I know this man hurt so many of us but I'm sure there was a boy in the body crying out for help. When he spoke to my daughter she told me he spoke like one of the kids at her school "she said". The Lord knew that my daughter was coming home and God allowed my daughter to listen to him and Allen opened up to my Morgan. You see Allen been crying for help all of his life and never got the help he needed. I hope you can enjoy the good times that he brought on us. And I'm sure he brought some of you guys happiness thank you "she added then she walk off the panel". She left that panel and didn't look back.

The following Sunday Debra, Robert, Sherry, and Momma Jones went to church getting out of their cars. They all greeted and they smiled at each other as they proceed to walk in the building.

THE REASON FOR DEBRA JONES

Well for most of you who don't me I'm a local rapper from Hot Springs Arkansas. I've been doing music for a while and decided to write this story. My music always been hardcore so I picked the most sensitive topic that I have seen growing up. I'm a brother of four sisters and been around domestic violence, infact I done prison time for one of them shooting her abusive boyfriend. And though he lived I could have been doing a life sentence for my actions, but instead I got a five year sentence. The point of the story is that no matter the situation violence should be the absolute last resort. I seen guys that were there for killing over women that still moved on to find new men.

Debra is a totally made up story and me as the writer had leave Pookie Bluffini the rapper to write this. For all the people that support my books I promise to give you more because you deserve it. And I hope that you will support them like most of you did with my albums over the years.

LIFE AS POOKIE BLUFFINI

Pookie Bluffini was built because I was a young rapper that wanted to stand out so not only I was super hardcore I wanted my name to stand out. I started a movement in Hot Springs because the younger artists loved the character and it gave them not only hope but a picture to build on. I wrote my rhymes as movies not stuff to act on. Terminator was a movie I liked growing up but I didn't take it literally. Pookie Bluffini is more like a character that was built off of the real me. I wanted to build careers so other people can benefit off of Pookie Bluffini.

I love to write and promise to deliver even more of Pookie Bluffini. But will admit this artist is not for everyone.

Shady Music Buisness

I'm an independent rap artist that tried to work with a lot of local acts. Because in our city the local rap labels were shady and all ways made money off of artists then refused to pay them. I watched a local artist sell his music on the streets then gave the money to the shady CEO. I've also dealt with a shady dude like that. He stole a lot from me and still wanted me to help him build his label.

Pookie Bluffini stood for the freedom of an artist. I will never deal with that person again unless he pays me what he owes me. But once I get the music back jumping I will help the entire local rap scene.

To the shady cats out there stealing from me with them online sells. Keep doing you because you will not **win.**